This book belongs to...

Just Like Jasper!

Nick Butterworth and Mick Inkpen

A division of Hachette Children's Books

Jasper is going
to the toyshop
with his birthday
money.

What will
he buy?

Will he choose
a ball?

Or perhaps a clockwork mouse?

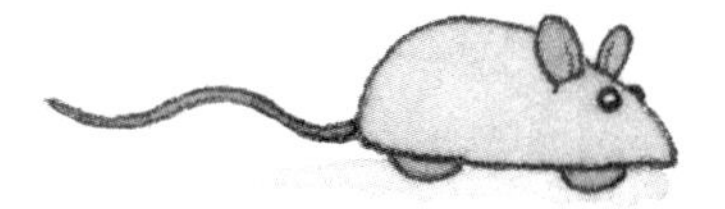

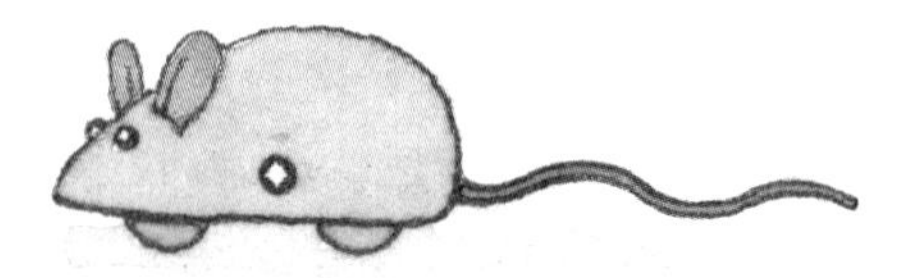

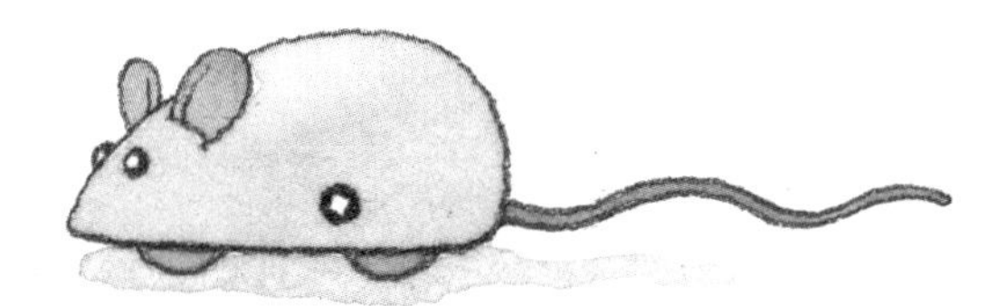

A noisy drum?

Or some bubbles?

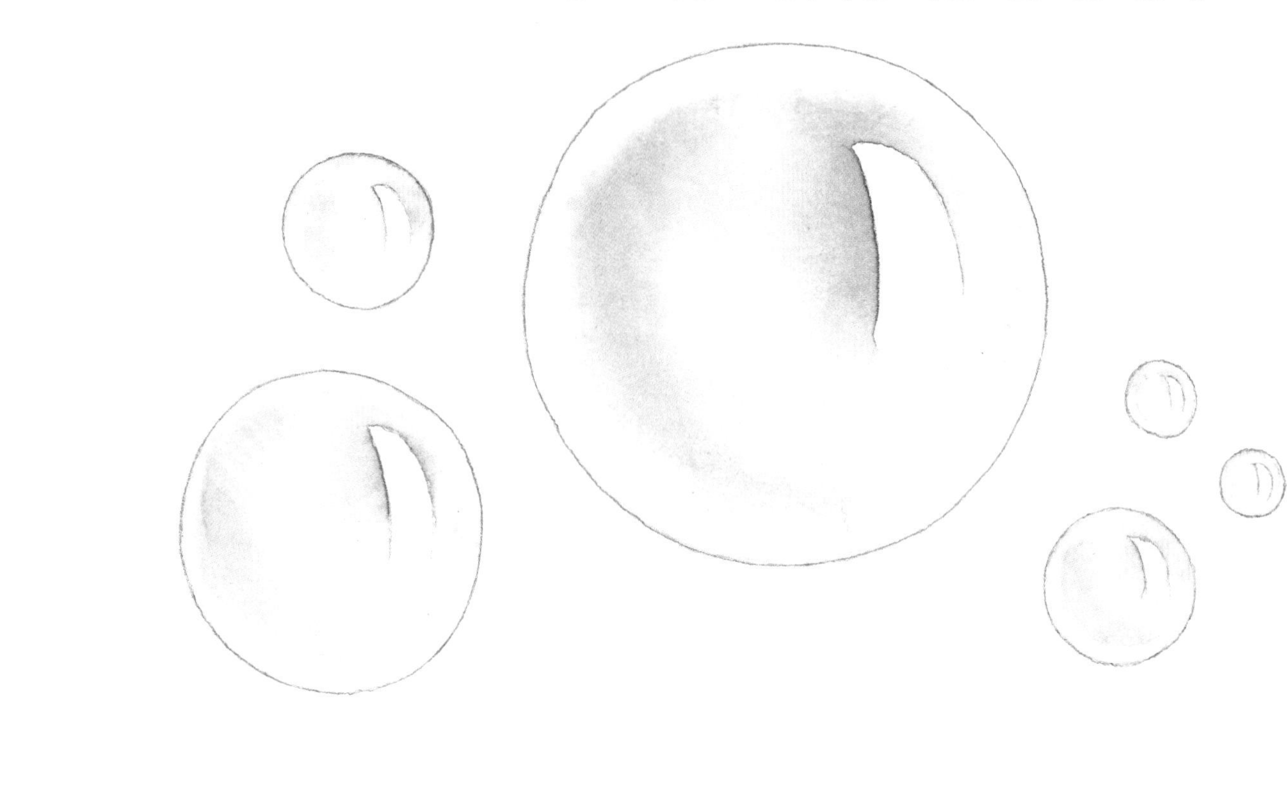

Would he like a car?

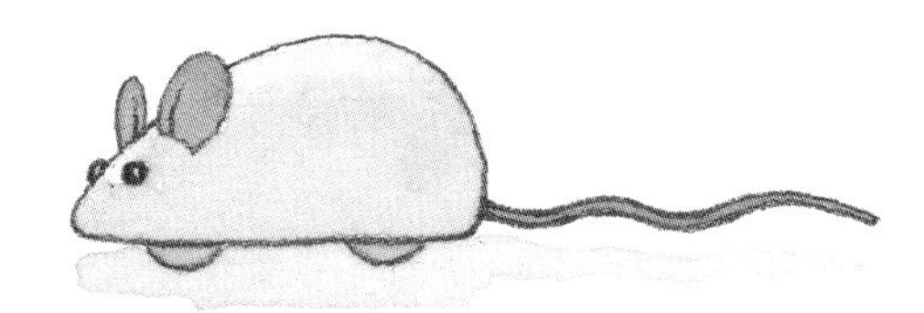

Or maybe a doll?

Or a robot?

Will he choose
a Jack-in-a-box?

No. Jasper doesn't want any of these.

What has he chosen?

It's a little cat.
Just like Jasper!

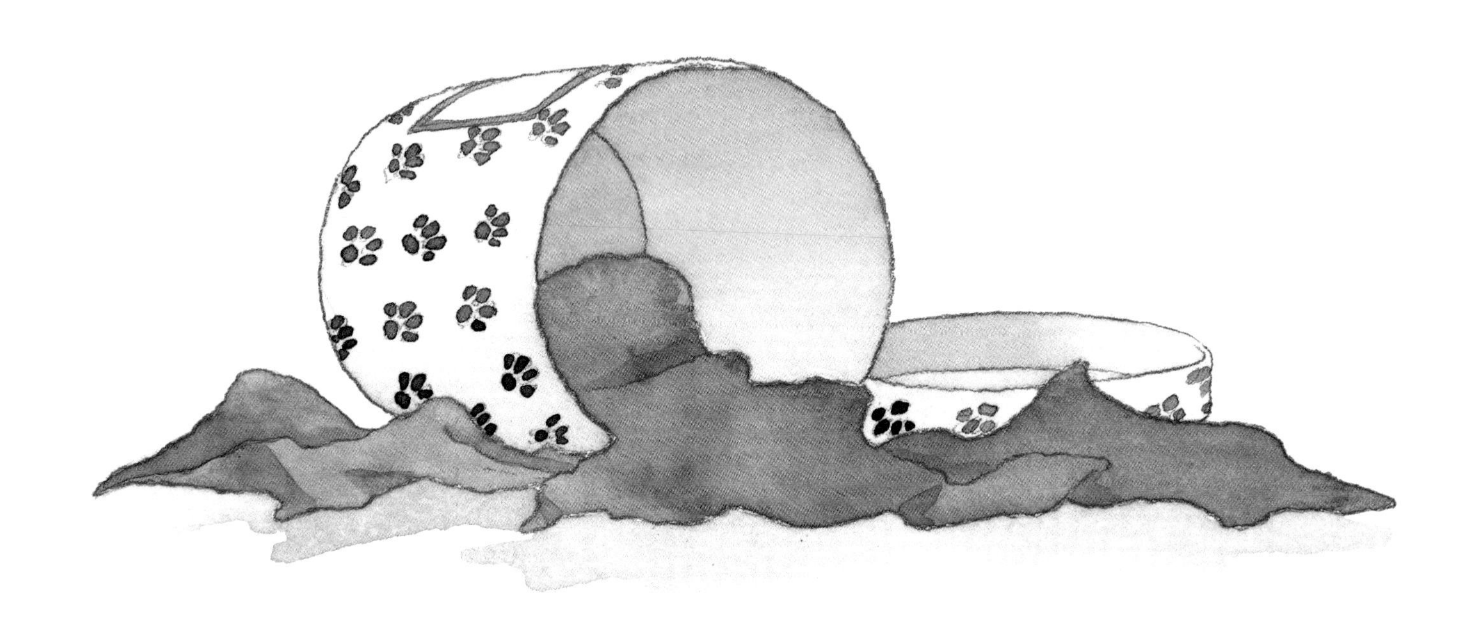

First published in 1989 by Hodder Children's Books

This edition published in 2008

Hodder Children's Books
338 Euston Road, London NW1 3BH

Hodder Children's Books Australia
Level 17/207 Kent Street, Sydney, NSW 2000

A catalogue record of this book is available from the British Library.

ISBN: 978 1 444 94423 5

Printed in China
Hodder Children's Books is a division of Hachette Children's Books,
an Hachette Livre UK Company